Rowan's Blood

by

Chris M. Carmichael

Proexemplar Publishing

Copyright 2012 © Chris M. Carmichael

ISBN-10: 0-9766736-6-5

ISBN-13-: 978-0976673668

This book is dedicated to all who see the world with the heart and soul and not just with the eyes.

ACKNOWLEDGMENTS

Much gratitude goes to all friends who have showed loving support and unconditional love along the way. You are angels on earth.

CHAPTER 1

The stench of charred flesh clutched at my throat through the icy night air. I retched as I ran but did not dare slow my steps. There was no time. The screams from the pyres pierced the night and my heart, the terrible sound urging me to move faster. I ran blindly through the dark forest, branches and briars tearing like claws at my clothes. It was as if even the trees had condemned me and sought to trap me.

Rowan followed behind me and had difficulty keeping up, but I made sure she did not fall too far behind. When she stumbled over a fallen branch, I grasped her hand, and tugged her quickly, silently to her feet. There was no time for words. The men chasing us grew closer with each breath.

Up ahead, a soft glow revealed where the forest gave way to moonlit cliffs. The sound of waves rushing against land pulsed in my ears; the faint salty scent of the sea mingled with the odor of the night's atrocities.

We slowed as we approached and stopped near the cliff edge. I scanned the area for the best passageway out of the moonlight, one that would take us further away from the men and would keep us well hidden. To my left I saw an opening in a distant line of trees and grasped Rowan's hand to lead her there, but she stood fast.

"Koren, go on and leave me here. I am slowing you down. Please."

"No! I won't leave here without you!"

She pressed her palm to my cheek. The moonlight on her blonde hair made it glow ghostly white. My heart clenched with panic and I tugged at her hand again to pull her with me, but she shook her head. In a shaky voice, she begged me, "Please, please, I cannot bear watching you die because of me. Leave now. Do this for me!"

The men's shouts grew louder. They were nearing the edge of the forest and soon would see us, if they had not already.

Rowan withdrew her hand and took a step back, "I promise I will always love you. Please remember my love for you."

I had no time to stop her as she took another step and threw herself over the cliff into the dark, churning sea far below. Horrified, I could not move or breathe for a long moment. Only when I heard a male voice shouting, did I find the will. I first ran away from the cliffs, towards the opening in the tree line that I had seen moments before. But then, driven by dark sorrow, I headed back towards the sea to join Rowan in the watery grave.

Rough hands stole my choice just moments before I reached the edge. They grabbed me and flung me down hard onto the cold rocky ground.

"We've got her, Jona!" A man's voice roared above me. They circled me like a pack of wolves as Jona approached. He stared down at me and then spat.

"Bring her back to the village," he ordered.

Three of the men reached down to grab me and pull me to my feet, but I refused to aid their attempts and let my body go limp and heavy. I made them drag me. I would not make this easy for them in any way. I knew death was imminent, and I had nothing more to lose. As they pulled me through the forest, they cursed me, but the words had no effect on me anymore.

I kept my eyes closed tightly, but the lingering odor of burned flesh let me know when we had arrived at the village.

"Take her to my cottage. I wish to deal with her myself in private," Jona said.

"As is your right," one of the men replied.

When they dragged me past the smoldering pyres, Jona made them stop. Reaching down to me, he grabbed my hair and forced my head back. He ordered me to open my eyes and look upon blackened remains hanging on the iron stakes.

"Take a good look, witch, a good, long look at

what your vulgar ways have brought you and your kin."

My heart beat dully in my chest. The weight of my grief wrapped around me, smothered me. I said nothing. After a few moments, Jona ordered the men to continue and they took me into his cottage to deposit me on the hard-packed dirt floor.

Lying still, and with my eyes tightly closed, I listened as the men left and then to the familiar sound of Jona's footfalls as he entered the cottage. I sensed him leaning over me and heard his breathing. He grabbed my wrists, pulled me roughly to my feet and shoved me down onto a wooden chair.

"Open your eyes!"

I opened them and stared past him, to the far wall. My life was forfeit, I knew this, and it did not matter anymore. He had killed all of them -- my family, my friends, and my beloved Rowan.

Jona paced in front of me, silent for a moment. The fetid odor of his sweat and aura of his hatred filled the small room. When he erupted again, spittle sprayed from his lips as he spoke.

"You were once my betrothed! You were promised to me! We were to start a life together! But you destroyed it all to follow that bitch's evil ways!"

I raised my head and saw rage twisting his features as he continued.

"And all of them," he paused and pointed towards the doorway, "all of those who hang silent now on the stakes, their blood is on your hands."

His words broke through the numbness inside of me and, in that moment, I hated him more than I could have dreamed possible, and more than I imagined one person could hate another and still breathe.

"Oh no, Jona. Don't you dare place blame for your evil on me! Their blood is on *your* hands! All of them are innocents. Every one of them. And you slaughtered them, just as you wish to slaughter me. I have done nothing."

Jona struck me so hard across the face I nearly fell off the chair.

"Nothing?" He bellowed. You and that witch, now dead in the sea, infested almost the entire village with your vile words and deeds."

He struck me again. Pain seared through my nose as it broke with a loud pop. Blood poured forth and ran in a steady, warm stream down to my chin. I tried to wipe it all away with my sleeve, but the flow was too heavy.

"Jona," I said quietly, "I did nothing wrong. Unless love is wrong. I did nothing wrong."

"Love? He screeched. "Love? And what of me, woman. What of the lying tongue of yours that proclaimed love for me?"

I said nothing.

"So you think you loved her? You call that abomination love?"

I forced myself to meet his eyes as I answered, "I once loved you; you were like a brother to me. My love for Rowan is different, but the love is not wrong. And healing others as we did in the manner of the old ways is neither evil nor wrong. You claim your actions honor a god, but what you and the others have done tonight is the biggest blasphemy and affront to any real god," I said.

Without warning, he lunged and hammered his fists into my face, and then he shoved me so hard I went sprawling to the floor. His heavy boots met my stomach and ribs again and again. With each kick he cursed me, his shouts drowning out my cries of pain. When I gagged on my own blood, he grabbed me by the arms, pulled me to my feet and slammed me against the stone wall.

He gripped my shoulders to keep me on my feet and glared into my eyes, his face only inches from mine.

"I give you one final chance to change your fate tonight. Deny your love for her, and we can leave this village and live out our lives together as it was meant to be."

A moment passed while I tried to gather strength to speak. Waves of nausea shook me and my vision was fading. Mustering all the power I had left, I shook my head slowly. "I cannot speak falsely. I cannot, I will not, deny my love for her."

Jona exploded. In one swift movement, he stepped back from me, unsheathed the sword at his side and plunged it into my abdomen. He gave one more rage-filled growl before he ran out of the cottage. I slumped to the floor.

∞

I do not know how long I lie there as life poured from me in sticky rivers of blood. Breathing was torturous; each movement of my chest sent excruciating jolts through me. In vain, I tried to pull the sword out to ease the pain, but I was too weak. Eventually, unconsciousness blessedly pulled me down, giving me temporary peace.

When I stirred again, I believed myself to be in a dream, at first. Glenna, an old woman I had not seen since I was a child, was kneeling over me. She looked tenderly at me and placed a finger to her lips, to let me know I should make no sound.

"I am going to help you, dear one," She said softly. "You won't die this night. And someday, you will find your Rowan again."

Glenna turned her attention to the sword in my belly. She grasped it by the hilt and pulled it out of me with one hard tug. New pain shot through me, forcing a gasping cry from my throat, but the old woman remained calm, even as fresh blood poured from the wound to pool around my body.

7

She cast me a look full of compassion while pulling a dagger from her skirts. With the blade, she cut her own flesh on her arm and let her blood drip into my wound. After a few heartbeats, she placed one hand on my chest and one hand on the sword, and began to chant in a language foreign to me.

CHAPTER 2

United States, October 2011

The earthy odor of decaying leaves mingled with the sweaty scent of young men and women in a hurry. From my bench perch near the University's liberal arts building, I watched the students as they walked past and I quietly drew in a long breath. If I focused, I could detect the cologne or perfume they wore, the detergent they used, and the amount of alcohol they consumed the previous night, plus much more.

Occasionally, one would glance my way, aware I was watching. Few paid attention to me, however. To them I was just another twenty-something year old woman, dressed in jeans and a black blazer; most of them probably assumed I was a student or a young member of the faculty.

Sometimes my hair was blonde; other times it was red or dark brown. That day, my hair was my natural color, dark brown, to which I had recently added a few auburn highlights, and it hung loose around my shoulders. I had felt too tired and hungry to do more than run a brush through it that morning.

I had been sitting there for nearly half an hour before a young woman with a mousy brown ponytail caught my attention. Her gait was timid and unsure. She looked down at the ground as she walked and held a textbook tightly to her chest. Next to her, an attractive, petite red-haired girl chatted about a test.

I arose and followed them. For the shy girl that day, I would be nothing more than a strange dream. For me, she would be a tonic to quell the growing fatigue and craving inside me.

After we entered a large brick building that housed the physics department, I touched her shoulder lightly and she turned to look into my eyes. I did not have to say anything; my gaze captured her and drew her to me. She told her friend she would see her later, and followed me into a restroom.

After taking her gently by the wrist, I led her to a vacant stall. There I pulled her into my arms and she succumbed easily, giving only one muffled cry as I bit into her. Afterwards, I held her to me and whispered words that would ensure she would not remember what I had done to her. I stayed with her until I was certain she would not faint, and then left her, with only a small mark on her neck as proof of what had happened.

Sated, I left the campus and wandered into the heart of the city to visit my favorite museums. I had been to them countless times, and they were as familiar as home to me. The artwork provided a pleasant, safe journey into others' lives and usually helped quiet my thoughts.

I had only been there for a short while, however, before I realized that things felt different. Even viewing my favorite paintings did not distract my mind from my own life. Soon, even the exhilaration of sated hunger faded and sadness drifted over me, settling like a pall over my heart.

I left the room I was in and walked to a newer exhibit. I hoped the change would lighten my mood, but there I found mostly paintings of women, and they reminded me of the girl and her gift to me, a gift that lasted too briefly. I longed for more.

Sometimes it had been more. Through the centuries, some had come to live with me, offering companionship and love, but inevitably the time always came when I had to send them back out into the world to avoid questions that I refused to answer. They lived, they aged, they died and I remained.

Depressed, I left the museums and returned to the

emptiness of my home, to be greeted by my only companion, a calico cat I called Jasmine. When I went to bed that night, it was with a heavy heart, unaware that my life was about to take an interesting turn.

∞

It happened the next morning as I sat on my usual bench and waited for my next opportunity for sustenance. Sunlight caressed the fallen leaves at my feet; I noted with mild interest how the autumnal colors of red, orange and yellow contrasted beautifully against my black boots. A few students wandered by, but none interested me any more than the leaves.

Just as I was about to give up and my thoughts turned towards leaving the campus, a chilly wind arose. When I reached to push back my hair that had blown over my face, the wind stopped and all grew still, as if the sky held its breath. A warm rush of energy washed over me then, flooding my veins and making my flesh tingle. I glanced around, and that is when I saw her.

She was getting out of a black car. Her manner of dress and general aura indicated to me she was not a student. I noted her dark suit and heels, her blonde hair, which she wore in a demure up do, and I let my gaze linger on her pale, delicate neck.

After she closed the car door, she began to walk down the path towards me, her strides confident and sure. The closer she drew, the more my skin tingled, as if mild electrical currents passed through me.

When she was only a few yards away a pang in my chest made my breath catch, but that feeling was soon replaced by a deep ache in the core of my belly. The feeling was similar to how I feel when feeding; it never happens otherwise.

Her eyes met mine and for a moment, I did not breathe. I felt seen in a way that felt so familiar and yet I had never experienced before. Something in her pale blue eyes went through to my soul and I could tell that she sensed something, too, because she halted. At least several seconds went by before she smiled gently and continued walking towards the liberal arts building.

She paused at the door and looked back at me. I tried to smile pleasantly, but I felt awkward and confused. After she disappeared from my sight, I exhaled. I had not even realized that I had been holding my breath again.

Students walked past me, but I paid no attention at all to them now. My mind was fully preoccupied. I felt revitalized, as if my hunger had been sated, and yet at the same time I felt a need that somehow went beyond that hunger. There was something about the woman, something pulling me to her. I did not know what it was, but I intended to find out.

CHAPTER 3

Through the university website, I learned that the blonde woman's name was Brianna Cheswick and that she was teaching medieval literature that year. The next day I went into her building and found her office. The door was open and inside she sat at her desk, peering down at piece of paper. She played with one strand of blonde hair, her slender fingers twirling it absently. I watched her in silence, confident in my ability to remain unseen when I choose.

To my surprise, she turned her head and looked right at me. It should not have been possible for her to notice me, not when I did not want her to, unless something odd was happening to me.

"Hello," she said.

"Hello."

She smiled. "May I help you?"

Her eyes bore into me and the longer our gaze held the more the energy between us grew. Her expression gradually softened, and then she blinked as if to shut out whatever feeling was passing between us.

When I finally found my voice, it sounded hollow and distant to my ears. "I was wondering if you'd mind if I sat in on one of your classes."

"That would be fine. Are you a student here?"

"Yes." It was a lie. "Thank you." I turned to leave but her voice stopped me.

"May I ask your name?"

Our eyes met again. I wanted to look away but found I could not.

"Koren Mackenzie." I told her my real name. I never do that.

"Well, Koren, I hope you'll enjoy it. When shall I expect you?"

"Tomorrow, professor."

"I am not a professor. You may call me Brianna, if you like." She stood from her desk and extended her hand. As I grasped it in mine, she smiled gently. "See you tomorrow then, Koren."

∞

When I left her office, I walked to a nearby park to gather my thoughts, but the park was as noisy that day as the university. Needing silence and solitude, I gave up and went home; there, I paced from room to room, as I often do when something is bothering me. Jasmine followed me at first, but soon grew bored and stretched out on a window ledge in the formal sitting room.

I spoke to her, my voice reverberating off the walls of the cavernous area. "What do you think, Jasmine? Who on earth is this woman and why does she have such an effect on me?"

Jasmine cleaned her paws, ignoring me completely. I left her and went out into the back garden to sit by the fountain.

I knew that it wasn't just that Brianna had slightly unsettled me; she had genuinely spooked me. No one had ever seen me when I didn't want him or her to see me except for… I inhaled sharply. *Except for Jona*. I rubbed my hand over the cool stone ledge of the pond and thought about the last time I had seen him. Jona had reincarnated three times and had somehow found me each time. Unlike me, he was mortal and easy to conquer, but the encounters were always very unpleasant. It had been almost a hundred years since I had last had to deal with him. By now, I hoped he had given up and moved on. Perhaps he had even finally found joy in a new life with someone … if so, at least it would keep him away from me.

My thoughts went back to Brianna and I briefly explored the possibility of her being a reincarnation of Jona, and then quickly dismissed it. Jona's presence was never pleasing, never felt right, and most certainly never caused the warmth this woman invoked in me.

A fish breached the water's surface next to me. I dipped my fingers into the pond and felt another fish kiss my hand.

"I bet you are hungry." I stood up. "Me, too."

CHAPTER 4

Brianna's class was held in a large auditorium. I chose a seat towards the back so that I would blend in with the other students more easily and not distract her. I wasn't sure if I'd be able to last the entire hour. I needed to feed again already, and being around so many people was sure to fuel the gnawing hunger inside of me. It was disconcerting and unusual -- I can usually go a week. It had only been two days.

Brianna entered the auditorium from the back and made her way up the center aisle. I felt her before I saw her and turned my head, catching her eye as she approached. She smiled down at me in acknowledgement, her light perfume and the clean scent of her clothing caressing me as she passed by. A torrid vision of her bare skin against mine flashed through me and I nearly gasped aloud.

The feeling of hunger tinged with carnal desire did not diminish the entire hour, but I remained to listen to her full lecture. When the class ended, I left quickly in search of easy prey. I chose an athletic-looking student who had sat in front of me. He had kind eyes, was soft and sweet, but in the end his essence did little to sate me.

Hot tears welled in my eyes after I left him, and I realized with astonishment that the tears were the first in hundreds of years. I knew in my heart that my disquiet had something to do with Brianna. Somehow, I had to see her again and learn more about her.

It was not until I got home that night that I finally realized what might be going on. It happened as I was washing the cat's bowl and looked down to see water splashing like waves against the stainless steel sink basin. At that moment, the memory of Rowan jumping from the cliff into the sea flashed before my eyes. My legs buckled at the image. Letting the bowl clatter into the sink, I clutched the countertop to keep myself from falling. *Oh god, of course. But, after all this time? Could Brianna be…?* As the centuries had passed, I had eventually given up on ever seeing Rowan again.

Jasmine padded into the kitchen to investigate the noise and brushed against my leg. Just as I looked down at her, a cold breeze washed over me, causing the hairs on the back of my neck to stand up. She jumped to the side and stared wild-eyed at something invisible to me, then hissed loudly before running out of the room.

A heavy, suffocating presence filled the space then and brought with it the pungent odor of burning flesh. Gagging, I leaned over the sink and vomited once.

Behind me, a male voice whispered my name, but when I turned around there was no one there. Then, just as quickly as it had come, the odor vanished and the heaviness lifted.

CHAPTER 5

I slept fitfully, waking often to horrible images flashing through my mind. The burning odor had not returned, but the effects on my psyche remained; it had opened a doorway in my spirit I had long ago closed. When the first light of morning came, the sun did little to vanquish the shadow that had fallen over my soul. I sensed that seeing Brianna again might be the only thing that could help and quickly rolled out of bed to shower and get dressed.

Later, when I arrived at the university, I spotted her almost immediately. She was walking a distance away, but she was not alone, so I held back and did not approach her. I let my eyes take her in and felt my throat tighten.

As if sensing me, she glanced my way, tilted her head and threw me a smile. I tried to smile back, but it may have looked more like a grimace.

∞

That afternoon I went to her office. The door was shut, but I could feel her on the other side and so I knocked. Her voice softly beckoned me to enter and I did, closing the door behind me.

"Hello Koren," she said without looking up, startling me again with her ability to sense me.

"I just wanted to drop by and say I enjoyed your class very much. Thank you for letting me sit in," I said.

She picked up three pens from her desk and deposited them in her briefcase. "I looked up your name. It doesn't list you as a student here," she replied. There was no anger or accusatory tone in her voice. She looked at me.

Meeting her gaze, I said, "Because I am not. I am sorry I lied. I feared you would not let me attend if you knew."

She smiled. "It's not at all a problem. I don't mind at all."

Again that intensity in her smile and eyes. I cleared my throat to suppress the feelings welling in me, feelings I was sure showed and so I looked away.

"Do you need a drink of water?"

I shook my head. "No, I am fine, thank you."

We shared a moment of awkward silence before she looked at her watch. "Wow. It's already 6 o'clock. Can you believe that? Close to dinner."

Well, that's it, I thought, *she is quietly dismissing me.*

"Yes, I didn't realize it was so late... I guess I should be going."

I turned to leave but she spoke again, asking, "Do you have plans? Would you like to join me some place for dinner?"

I hesitated for a moment too long and she took it the wrong way. When I turned around, I saw her cheeks were flushed and she was avoiding my gaze. She gathered papers on her desk and shoved them into a leather briefcase, while saying, "Oh I meant if you have other plans that is okay of course." Her tone had softened and acquired a perceptible tremor."

"No," I said, "I would love to. When? Tonight?"

She looked up at me, a hint of a smile playing on her lips and nodded. "Yes, if you aren't busy."

Inwardly I rolled my eyes at myself. Of *course* she had meant tonight.

∞

We chose an Italian place not far from the university. The restaurant was pleasantly quiet and dark. Red wine sparkled in clear glasses, illuminated by candle light.

The food was not simply delicious, it was ambrosial, but eating was really not one of my needs at that moment. I craved much more, more than the delicate woman across from me could even imagine, and I was glad she could not imagine it because I was sure it would terrify her. I pushed my pasta gently with my fork as I thought of this. The last thing I wanted to see was fear in her eyes. If Brianna *were* Rowan, what would she think of what I had become?

Cold settled in the pit of my stomach. I tried to shove away the growing sadness that tore at my heart. Whether or not the woman sitting across from me was really Rowan, I felt very protective of her. The feeling was at once exhilarating and horrifying.

"Is your food okay?" Brianna asked quietly, unspoken concern showing in her tone and her eyes, as she sensed my mood change.

"Yes, it is heavenly. I am just not as hungry as I thought, I guess. How is yours?"

"It's wonderful. This is a nice place." She sat her fork down and took a sip of wine before continuing. "You know Koren, this may sound funny, but you just seem so familiar. I cannot put my finger on why, but you do."

I told her I felt the same way. She smiled at me and just said "funny, isn't it?"

I nodded in agreement and, for the moment, we left it at that.

Changing the subject, she asked where I was from. I couldn't tell her the entire truth, but did tell her I was from Scotland originally. I said my family had moved to the States when I was very young.

Her eyes lit up at the news. When she told me she had always felt drawn to visit Scotland, I said impulsively, "Well, perhaps we can take a trip sometime," although I knew in my heart that it was the last place on earth I wanted to take anyone to, considering the horrible memories it held.

Brianna appeared delighted at the idea of a trip together. "I would love that!"

When we finished the meal and waited for the check, Brianna caught my eye from across the table.

She lifted her wine glass. "I know it is getting late, but if you are up for it, would you like to continue this at my house? I have plenty of wine and some spirits," she said.

The invitation came as a surprise, and I was nearly beside myself with the need to find real sustenance again, nevertheless I did not want to miss the opportunity to discover more about her. I told her that I would love to continue our conversation at her place.

CHAPTER 6

Fat drops of rain splashed against the windshield as I drove us to her home, and when I pulled into her driveway, the sky opened up to unleash a torrent of cold rain. We had to sprint from the car to her front door to avoid getting drenched. Nervous and in a hurry, Brianna fumbled with her keys, but at last the door swung opened and we rushed inside.

Warmth met me as I stepped from the foyer into her front room. The house was small but the dark wood furnishings made it cozy and welcoming, and this feeling was enhanced by its contrast to the cold storm brewing outside. I appreciatively noted how Brianna had taken care to create a comfortable atmosphere for herself, despite the fact that she had not been in the area long and did not know if she would remain there.

She placed her coat on a coat rack and took mine too. "Would you like a glass of wine? Or something else? I have vodka, bourbon and mixers."

"Wine would be perfect, thank you."

After inviting me to relax on the sofa, she disappeared into another room then re-emerged in minutes with a small carafe of red wine and two glasses, which she placed on the coffee table. She poured the wine and handed a glass to me, a smile glinting in her eyes.

I sipped the wine slowly, savoring it. "This is very nice, thank you."

"I have several in there, but this is an Italian."

I asked if she had ever been to Italy. When she told me she had not, I told her about some of the places I had been, particularly Rome. Brianna kept our glasses filled while we discussed other places we had been and all the places we would love to see. The conversation also gave me the opportunity to waylay inevitable questions about my finances by explaining my inheritance. It was partly true. Throughout the years, I had acquired a measurable sum of wealth, but it had nothing to do with my family.

∞

The clock on the wall chimed softly. Almost two hours had already passed by the time our conversation switched from travel to subjects that were more intimate. The wine was finally loosening Brianna's tongue. "

"Have you ever been married?" she asked.

I shook my head. "No. Have you?"

She shook her head and so I asked the next obvious question, about whether she had anyone special in her life. Again the answer was no.

"I bet you get a lot of offers, "I said, "you are very beautiful."

A hint of crimson colored her cheeks. She gave a little laugh and then looked up from her glass, into my eyes. It was not difficult to detect her feelings, which were the same as mine.

Abruptly she looked away and took another sip of her wine. I noticed her hands were trembling. "I was going to say something similar to you," she said softly. "I figured you must have men, or women, after you all the time."

"I haven't been in any kind of relationship in a long time," I replied.

The air between us immediately grew pensive and anticipatory. Brianna turned her attention to the empty glasses and carafe, and avoided my gaze.

"Out of wine -- I should get more," she murmured then stood to go to the kitchen. I arose as well, offering to help her and she turned suddenly to me.

"I think I have only a pinot noir and a Shiraz left at the moment, "she said quickly. " Do you have a preference?" She looked down at the carafe in her hands. "Also, if you are hungry I could fix us something to eat – I know you didn't really eat much at the restaurant." She began to say something else but I touched her arm, and she looked up into my eyes again and grew silent.

"Are you okay?" I asked. A flush crept over her cheeks, but she nodded.

I touched her face lightly with my fingertips. "You sure?"

She took a step closer, her gaze never leaving mine as she reached up to my hand and pressed it to her cheek. "Yes."

My pulse beat wildly in my throat as we both grew very still, aware of the energy that surged between us. It burned through my hand on her cheek, through her eyes that drew me in, and through her scent, which changed almost imperceptibly. Only the sound of softly rolling thunder disturbed the silence that had fallen over us.

Her fingertips sensually caressed the back of my hand and her expression spoke of invitation, of love, and desire, but I did not wish to make presumptions. I resisted pulling her into my arms and simply leaned to place a gentle, tentative kiss on her cheek. But she turned her head so that our lips met instead. Warm, soft, her mouth pressed gently to mine in a lingering kiss that left us both breathless.

She stepped closer and kissed me again, parting her lips slightly this time and yielding to me when I pressed harder. A muffled moan escaped her throat and I felt a tremor chase through her body, but then she pulled back suddenly and I worried I had been too bold.

My concern vanished when she looked at me and I saw the deep emotion and longing that darkened her beautiful eyes.

Our breath mingled for a delicious moment before she smiled tenderly, nuzzled my cheek, kissed my earlobe, and then set the carafe down on the coffee table.

When she turned back to me, her eyes were sparkling. Wrapping her arms around my neck, she pulled my face down to her, her lips parting again in welcome as I pressed my mouth to hers. A low growl of thunder rolled across the sky outside again as, inside, I claimed her soft lips, tasting and exploring her gently, but thoroughly.

Her hair was silk against my hand as I gently grasped it, guiding her. She pressed tightly to me, a whimper escaping her throat as I coaxed her desire steadily forth with each breath, each moan, and each caress of my tongue against hers. Soon, we were both dizzy from passion and had to break the kiss if only to breathe. Brianna rested her face against my neck, with her arms still wrapped around me. I could feel her heartbeat solidly against me. She planted one soft kiss on my cheek before whispering, "Take me to bed."

∞

Lightening flashed through the bedroom window, illuminating us as we stood facing each other. Brianna's touch trailed up my arms, to my shoulders as I drew her to me and claimed her soft lips again in a kiss full of growing desire.

Needing desperately to feel more of her, I boldly slipped one hand under her shirt to caress skin, hot and silky soft. Whimpering into my mouth, she pressed her body hard to me and grasped the back of my head, forcing my lips harder to hers.

Passion pulsed, burned, and nearly sent us reeling as our knees buckled. I guided her quickly to the bed before we fell. There, passion unleashed itself in a fury. In between kisses, our hands worked impatiently to remove clothing, so that warm skin would meet warm skin and discover what the kisses had promised. Finally free of any barriers, she arched to me, pulling me down against her luscious softness, her hands clutching at my back. Thunder rumbled louder outside, the sound competing with our moans.

I moved my hand down to grasp her hip and pressed harder to her. A bone-jarring shudder jolted me as I felt her tremble beneath me. I had to fight an impulse to take her roughly and immediately. I wanted to savor the moment, and reined in my desire to keep some control.

I lifted from her mouth to breathe, to look at her again, and to know this was real, for it felt like a beautiful dream. Even in the dim light, I could see her clearly and the love in her eyes made me feel my heart would burst. As she smiled the softest of smiles, she stroked my spine and shoulder blades, her fingernails grazing the skin and sending shivers of pleasure through me.

I could not hold back a low moan as she closed her eyes and arched against me.

Leaning down again, I kissed her shoulder, tasting salty skin. She turned her head, instinctively offering her neck, innocent to what this would do to me. I groaned as my stomach clenched and my mouth watered, anticipating the coppery sweet taste of her blood. I knew I had to battle the fierce hunger threatening to overtake me. I sensed that I would not be able to stop if I gave into it, and would go too far.

Repressing the hunger made me shudder.

Brianna responded by pressing her hands tightly to my back. "I want you," she said, her breath hot against my neck. "Please."

"I don't want to hurt you," I said

"You won't," she said, and grasped my hand to press it to her breast. "Please."

"Oh god."

Heat exploded between us. Even if we had wanted to stop, at that point there was no going back. Brianna arched her neck to me again, inviting my mouth and this time I gave in as much as I dared. Kissing and sucking the skin just below her earlobe, I moaned feeling her yield in surrender to me.

Her breath caught then came in short gasps as I slid my hand from her breast down her stomach, then lower, to find her need. With a loud cry, she lifted her hips to me then turned her head to kiss me hard, moaning loudly into my mouth and sucking on my tongue.

Outside, the thunder roared as the storm exploded through the sky. Inside, my blood pounded in my ears and my vision blurred from a craving that had me on a dangerous edge. I closed my eyes tightly to force the feeling away, but images of Rowan flashed through me, her face, her eyes, her mouth, her voice pleading with me. Then the voice was Brianna's, pleading as she broke the kiss and threw her head back against the pillows, her fingernails digging into my back urging me to take her.

Lightning flashed again, illuminating her pale form. The beautiful image crumbled most of my resolve and before I could stop myself, my mouth was on her neck. Her pulse throbbed just beneath the skin, taunting me, telling the tale of hot blood just beneath the surface, waiting for me. Groaning, I summoned all the power I had, and forced myself to turn away from her neck and press my face into the sheets next to her head.

I directed the power of my need and desire towards exploring and taking the many other gifts she offered me. Piercing cries tore from her throat, as my touch grew stronger and more commanding.

As I pushed harder against her, finding her core, I summoned her surrender, touched her soul, and filled her with mine. With a violent shudder, she gave a final loud cry before falling limp and gasping beneath me.

∞

In the morning, I awoke to her warm body pressed tightly to me. Caressing her hair, I inhaled her beautiful scent as she stirred. She blinked sleepily at me, and then pressed her face into my shoulder while murmuring something that sounded like "I love you." It was too muffled for me to be certain.

"Hmm?"

Pulling back a little, she smiled sweetly. "Good morning."

CHAPTER 7

Sunlight streamed through my study window and danced off dust particles in the air. I leaned back in my chair, closed the leather-bound volume of Chaucer's works I'd been half-heartedly reading, and let it rest on my lap. It was mid afternoon, one month after the first night I had spent with Brianna. She was at the university working and I was trying to get my mind off my hunger.

Becoming intimate with her had changed me, but the changes were not all good. My need for blood had increased profoundly, as did the painful effects when I did not sate the need often enough. This once meant finding someone once or twice a week. After meeting Brianna, it meant daily, at minimum. That we spent so much time together added to the tension. I continued to avoid using her to sate that particular need, and sneaking off to find others was not always easy, especially on the weekends when she wanted to spend days and nights together.

In addition, I'd intended to take our new relationship slowly, but Brianna's beautiful energy, her intense passion and loving attention towards me, made it difficult to keep that resolve. Nevertheless, I tried, for I knew from all my time on earth that rushing into anything can yield unpleasant results.

I worried Brianna would lose herself too quickly in this before she was really prepared to handle it – especially since she did not yet know my secret. I was acutely aware that our relationship was easier for me, and less confusing, because unlike Brianna, I had at least a clue why we had such strong feelings for each other. I was not completely convinced that she was Rowan reincarnated, but I was mostly convinced.

I was thinking about this when my mobile phone chimed, alerting me that I'd received a text message. I was surprised to see that it was from Brianna, as she usually preferred to call: *'Are you busy? If not, could you stop by my office for a moment?'*

Twenty minutes later, I was on campus, making my way quietly through the throngs of students. When I arrived at her office door, it was closed. I knocked softly.

"Yes, enter," she said.

Brianna was staring down at a student paper. Other papers covered her desk and lay messily, as if thrown there, which went against her usual orderliness. She looked up from her work, her eyes were red-rimmed as if she'd been crying, and she appeared exhausted.

"Everything okay?" I asked.

"Yes," she said, although her tone conveyed otherwise. "I wondered if you would like to grab something to eat and we could take it back to my place for an early dinner. I am not keeping late office hours this afternoon."

We picked up Thai cuisine on the way to her home. Brianna ordered one of her favorite dishes, but later when we settled down at her dining room table, I noticed she was merely picking at the food.

"I can tell something is up, love. What is wrong?"

She offered an apologetic smile. "I'm sorry; I just didn't sleep well last night. I had a terrible nightmare." She put her fork down and exhaled. "It was just awful and I haven't been able to shake the feeling all day. I know it is stupid."

"Maybe it will help if you tell me about it?"

After taking a few sips of wine, she relayed the dream to me, in detail. My heart clenched. It was not just a dream she was describing. She was conveying Rowan's final moments, from Rowan's perspective.

Fresh tears shone in her eyes as she finished and her voice broke. Quickly, I went to her side. "Let's go into the other room, sweetheart," I said and led her to the sofa, where she curled tightly into my arms and began to cry quietly into my shoulder. I wanted to say something to soothe her, but words would not come. It was too difficult. I *did* want to tell her that I am that woman she saw, but it was no dream and I have been alive all these hundreds of years... alive because an old woman did something that spared me from a natural death.

But, I could not tell her. I was not prepared to do that yet. I needed time to figure out how to tell her without it hurting her or frightening her.

When her tears subsided, she said quietly, "You probably think I am like a silly school girl now, being so affected by a dream like that."

"No, I don't think that of you. Not at all."

"It is just… it was so terrifying, Koren. And you… I felt so much love for you and so much sorrow because I knew I would never see you again. I was so afraid for your life, so afraid to watch you die. I couldn't bear it. Then there was that feeling of falling. I just kept trying to scream."

"I don't think it is silly. It sounds horribly frightening."

She snuggled closer and rested her head against my chest. My heart was pounding and I wondered if she could feel it. I felt I had to say something.

"Brianna… do you believe in reincarnation?"

She lifted her head up and I felt her looking at me, but I studied the far wall and didn't meet her gaze.

"I don't know but I'd like to think it is possible," she said, "Why? Do you?"

"Yes," I said.

"So, you think that dream could be a past life memory?"

"Yes, because I've had similar dreams." It hurt me to say it, because it was a half-lie, but until I knew what else to say, it would have to do. Finally, I looked at her again. Her eyes were swollen from crying and my heart ached for her.

She reached one hand up and stroked my face. "Tell me about your dreams, please."

The warmth of her, the sound of her breathing helped me steady my voice as I began to tell her my half of the story. I told her a lot, but left out the most important part about the old woman coming to me when I lay broken and bleeding on the dirt floor. I did not dare say that I survived the night and had felt no physical pain from my wounds because they had already healed. I could not tell her what I became and how, grief stricken, I left the village that night and, eventually, left Scotland entirely.

Stillness hung over us as we both took in the feelings the memories brought. After a while, Brianna took my hand in hers, pressed my palm to her lips and then against her heart. "It makes a lot of sense," she said. "It would explain so much, wouldn't it? Like why I was drawn to you from the moment I first saw you, and how I feel that I have loved you forever."

Her words made my heart both soar and break. I felt her love, but she loved the human being she thought I was. It was difficult for me to believe that anyone, even Rowan, could love what I had become.

"I love you, too," was all I dared say in that moment.

CHAPTER 8

Lapis blue, emerald green, yellow ochre, Parisian blue and other colors blended on the canvas inches in front of me. As I stepped slowly back from the painting, the colors gradually gathered form. When I was a few feet away, I could discern the peacock the artist had painted hundreds of years before. Another museum patron stared at me from my left, but I didn't pay attention to her. Her curiosity reached over like snaking hands tugging at me, but I wasn't going to explain my behavior. I had my own ways of appreciating artwork and this was one of my favorite paintings.

We often forget the importance of perception and think that what we *see* is what *is*, but that is not so. Much depends on where one is in relationship to any particular thing at any given moment. The peacock painting remains a peacock painting, but wherever I stand in relationship to it makes a difference to how I respond to it.

Life is like that. We do not always know what we are really seeing unless we are in the proper alignment – which means we can easily make mistakes about what appears to be and respond inappropriately.

I folded my arms and stood very still. My thoughts drifted from the painting to Brianna. Final exam time had arrived for the university and that meant she had a bigger workload grading papers, which in turn meant we weren't seeing each other very much. Although I missed her terribly, it gave me time to step back and view our situation from different angles. My heart, my mind, and my intuition felt that we were meant to be together, and that it was far more probable that she was Rowan than not. However, the knowledge that someday I would have to tell her everything about me, or leave her, robbed me of the joy I would otherwise feel.

In addition, there was something beyond that, something I couldn't put my finger on but plagued me. It was a sense of foreboding.

"It is amazing that anything can retain so much beauty and vibrancy despite the centuries, isn't it?" A male voice said, startling me from my musing. I turned to see a well-dressed man in his 30's or early 40's looking at me with an appreciative smile.

"Yes," I said, "amazing."
"I think I've seen you here before. My name is Alex."

His eyes were an interesting shade of dark blue, perhaps enhanced by colored contacts; the way those eyes unabashedly studied me, I could tell he was used to getting what he wanted. I hid a bemused smile as I told him my name.

"Koren, that is an interesting name," he replied. "Do many people call you Korey instead?"

"Not if they want to live," I said.

He grinned broadly, displaying perfectly straight, white teeth. "So, Koren, are you an artist yourself or do you just enjoy looking at it."

I told him that I painted, but that it was purely for my own pleasure. Maintaining eye contact, I allowed the word '*pleasure*' to hang in the air between us. It had the desired effect. His smile changed and his eyes darkened with a trace of lust. Despite the boldness and, perhaps, arrogance I detected within him, he was going to be an easy catch, but it was not going to be the kind of intimate interaction he really wanted.

When he composed himself enough to speak, he invited me to go have a coffee with him. I accepted the invitation with a smile and began to walk with him, but as we walked past a restroom, I stopped, looked at him and took his hand.

He let me lead him. As soon as we were safely hidden in a stall, he wasted no time going for what he wanted. He assumed it was what I wanted, too, and of course I understood, but his roughness angered me.

When he tried to kiss me and slid his hand up my shirt to squeeze my breast, I grabbed his wrist. "No. Don't," I said, but he was impatient and did not stop. He pushed against me harder, his hand still roughly squeezing my breast, so I tightened my grip. "I said, no."

The skin yielded beneath my fingertips and his bones flexed, but he was not giving up. I gripped his wrist even harder, and wondered if I was going to have to break it before he stopped. It wasn't until the bones were just about to pop that he finally released my breast and stared at me, confused at my strength.

I shook my head slowly and directed him to turn his head. He groaned as I sunk my teeth into his neck until a fountain of blood poured into my mouth. My hunger was strong but so was he, so I allowed myself to give into the darker side of my craving and tore into him violently, drawing out as much as I could until he collapsed against me.

Sated, I left him sitting in the stall to recover and decided to leave the museum and go home. On the way out, however, I was drawn to look at another favorite painting.

It portrayed a common scene, a ship in a storm, but was ripe with detail. It was as if the waves would spill off the canvas at any moment, and barely visible in one corner, one could make out the outline of a sea creature cresting the waves.

As I lost myself in the artist's ocean, I felt a hand rest on my shoulder. I turned, expecting that Alex had already awoken and had somehow found me again, but no one was there. A shudder went through me as a heavy, suffocating presence filled the space around me.

Hot breath fell upon my neck as something whispered my name. I wanted to run, but tendrils of fear wrapped around me and locked me in place. The voice whispered my name once more and then, just as quickly as it had come, the presence left me alone... and unnerved.

∞

Jasmine met me at the door when I arrived home, but I did not stop to pet her. Instead, I headed straight for the shower. Alex's cologne and the feeling of the dark presence lingered on my hair and clothes and made me feel sick inside.

After I had scrubbed my skin raw, I put on a clean robe and, following an impulse, went to my art room. There I searched through the messy space until I came upon my first painting of Rowan. I had painted it before I had given up hope of ever seeing her again. Her blue eyes peered back at me from the canvas. Behind her lone figure, straw-colored grass gave way to beach sand and a lapis blue ocean.

I secured the painting on an easel and sat down in my chair to gaze at it. After a while, it was as if she were truly there looking back at me, and my throat tightened.

I spoke aloud to her, because the words needed to be said, even if she could not hear me.

"I never forgot you. I only gave up waiting because it seemed you were never coming back. I had to move on, because the pain was just too much. I relived that night so many times in my head, wondering if there was any way I could have saved you. I still do not know if I did the right things, if I did all I could. All I know is I loved you; I still love you and always will. I do not know who Brianna is, but if she is you then I will cherish her forever. If she is not, I will treat her right, because no matter who she is, she has a beautiful heart and deserves the best."

My throat clenched and my heart ached. Tears filled my eyes, but never fell. I sat there for a while longer in silence before leaving to go to bed.

CHAPTER 9

Jasmine brushed against my leg and meowed impatiently as I set the table and then followed me into the sitting room to watch as I lit a fire in the fireplace to cut the January chill. I was late feeding the cat her evening treat because I was busy preparing for Brianna's arrival.

That night would only be the third time she had ever been to my home, even though we'd been together over two months. After my experience in October with the presence in the kitchen, I hadn't felt it was entirely safe for her to come over. However, I knew that she would think it strange if I never invited her, especially since she really loved my home.

I had just put the catered food in the oven to keep it warm when the doorbell rang. As usual, she was on time. When I opened the door, my breath caught in my throat at the sight of her. She looked so much like Rowan in that moment. It was the brown cloak and the way she wore her hair, loose and falling around her face. For a few seconds, I just looked at her, unable to speak, until I saw her fidget with her handbag and realized that I was staring.

Wordlessly I stepped aside, inviting her to enter. Her boots made hollow sounds on the hardwood floor as she slowly stepped in past me. "Mmm, the food smells wonderful."

I helped her remove her cloak and watched as her hair fell in soft golden strands down her back. She turned to me and wrapped her arms around my neck. "I missed you," she said softly.

∞

We made only light conversation during dinner while we savored the food and each other's presence. The soft glow from the candles shimmered in her eyes as she looked at me from across the table. When she smiled tenderly, all my worries about our relationship temporarily vanished. In that moment, I felt that even if she knew my secret she would still love me.

After dinner, we sipped wine on the sofa near the fireplace. Brianna nestled into me, her head resting against my shoulder. I exhaled slowly, relaxing, until I felt her stiffen. I looked at her.

Her brow furrowed. "I just remembered parts of my dream… that's all."

"Because of the fire? We can go to another room, if you would prefer."

She shook her head. "No, it is beautiful in here, so peaceful. This is very nice." Placing her hand on my leg, she turned her head to kiss my cheek.

Later when we made love, it was slow, tender and more passionate than I had ever experienced. It was as if it was our first time together again, but imbued with new layers of love and affection we had developed towards each other. It was hours before we finally fell into deep sleep.

∞

Sometime in the very early morning, I woke to Brianna talking in her sleep. At first, I could not make out any of what she was saying, but then realized it was because she was speaking in our old tongue. "Oh Rowan," I whispered, "If I doubted at all before, I've no doubt now."

Brianna jerked; her voice grew louder and more urgent. I realized she was having a nightmare and shook her gently, but she was trapped in the dream.

"Brianna." I shook her harder. I repeated her name, but she did not awaken until I was nearly yelling.

She stared at me, confused, for a moment. "Koren?"

"Yes, I am here."

She pressed herself tightly into my arms. "I love you."

A loud crash that seemed to come from the kitchen startled us both then. I scrambled from the bed and grabbed my robe.

"Do you want me to come with you?" Brianna whispered.

"No, stay here."

I crept down the dark hallway, listening carefully. When I arrived at the kitchen, nothing appeared out of order. I listened for a moment more before quietly calling for Jasmine. She did not come. I repeated her name a little louder. When she still did not come, I told myself that the sound had probably spooked her and that she was hiding somewhere else in the house. Just as I started to leave to check the other rooms, a cold breeze washed over me.

"Koren." The voice was a ragged whisper, cavernous, inhuman, and familiar.

"Show yourself," I commanded.

"Show yourself," the voice mocked me.

I stared into the darkness. "Who are you?" I asked evenly.

It laughed. "You know who I am."

My temper flared. "I am not in the mood for games! Who the hell are you?"

"Jona," the voice answered. "We will see each other soon, Koren. Very soon."

The air stilled and the kitchen light in the kitchen came on by itself. The presence was gone. Exhaling, I leaned against the wall to compose myself before returning to the bedroom.

There I found Brianna sitting on the edge of the bed, the blanket wrapped around her. She looked terrified.

"What was it?" she asked.

"I think it was just the cat, honey, don't worry."

"I heard you talking?"

I let my robe fall to the floor and got back into the bed, immediately pulling her close.

"Don't worry about it. Everything's okay."

She let her head rest against my collarbone. I could feel her trembling. "Before that happened, I was having those dreams again," she said.

"I know."

"You do?"

"You were talking in your sleep." I rubbed her shoulder to relax her. "Just try to go back to sleep."

CHAPTER 10

When I woke again, I felt such intense hunger I groaned aloud before remembering Brianna was with me. She stirred and wrapped her arms around me, pressing her body to me tightly, but her scent and the feel of her heart pounding against me sent me to the edge. I pulled back from her before I lost myself to the temptation. She opened her eyes and looked at me.

Without a word, I left her alone on the bed, went into the bathroom and shut the door. I turned on the sink faucet and just let the water run, as I tried to regain some composure. Catching my reflection in the mirror, I grimaced at what I saw. My skin was grey and my eyes dull. I needed to feed, and soon.

I started to turn away but then my reflection changed in front of my eyes. Horror gripped me as purple and black bruises appeared beneath my eyes. An open sore marred my hairline. When wet warmth on my torso made me look down, I barely stifled a scream. Blood covered my abdomen, issuing slowly from a gaping wound.

Gripping the sink, I squeezed my eyes shut and told myself it was just an illusion, brought on my hunger. *Please let it be an illusion.* I breathed deeply trying to calm myself. Only after many long minutes did my pulse slow and only then did I open my eyes again. To my deep relief, I saw that the blood, the wounds, had all disappeared. I took a few more moments to gather myself before facing Brianna again.

Her gaze held me as I walked back to the bed, concern playing over her features. "Are you feeling okay?"

I tried to smile. "I'm fine."

She pulled back the blankets to welcome me into the warmth.

"Mmm that's better," she said and ran her hand up my rib cage, then pressed her mouth to my throat and let her tongue trace a hot path over the jugular. I moaned -- it was mostly from hunger, but she thought it was from sexual need and continued her seduction by sliding her leg over mine so I could feel the heat that was building between her thighs.

My stomach tightened. Brianna's carnal boldness was fueling the fury inside me that I had been trying to suppress. She had no idea what could be in store for her if she continued. When she moved her hand over my belly, it was too much. With a low growl, I turned and pinned her beneath me. She whimpered and looked into my eyes. "I need you."

A shadow fell over me and spread through my veins. It pulsed in my jaw, pumped fire through my limbs, clouded my vision and echoed from my throat in an otherworldly groan. I was only briefly aware of her mouth on mine. After that, the rush of furious need stole my senses and all I was aware of was the compulsion to take, to have, to demand and command.

∞

Much later, when the shadow lifted, I found myself sprawled on top of her. She was unconscious, facedown on the bed, her face turned to one side, with sweat-drenched strands of her hair loosely draped across her cheek and neck. Carefully, I lifted from her and rolled over to the side. I looked over her body for any signs of serious trauma; other than deep scratches and some bruising, I saw no injuries, but guilt and fear clutched my heart nonetheless.

CHAPTER 11

Later that day I apologized to Brianna for being rough. I did not mention that I did not even remember anything. A sexy smile crossed her face and she kissed my cheek. "No need to apologize."

I was relieved that she seemed okay and that she was not upset; however, I was very disturbed and heartsick that I had lost control with her. Even though I had not seriously hurt her, I knew it might only be a matter of time. I vowed to myself to find some way to prevent that, no matter what, so in the following months I chose extra prey to minimize my craving. Unfortunately, as I had feared would happen, Brianna eventually caught me in a situation.

A Goth girl was my undoing. She was instantly attracted to me and I barely had to seduce her at all. I found her in the library. She was reading Victorian erotica and she cast me a curious look as I walked past.

I sat down at a table nearby and pretended to read while I candidly felt her out. After the fourth time that I felt her eyes upon me, I went to her. We looked at each other silently for a few moments before I reached down, took the book from her hand and closed it, then extended my hand to her.

She allowed me to lead her to a corner restroom and there she gave herself to me. I took more from her than I usually allow myself, because she was so willing and had so much life energy to give. When I had finished, I was so pumped up from the rush that I almost forgot to eliminate her memory of it. It was only when she looked up at me, her eyes glassy with what looked like desire, and leaned forward to kiss me, that I remembered.

We left the restroom together, with her holding onto my arm, and that is when we ran into Brianna. She was just rounding the corner. I halted my steps as her eyes met mine.

"Koren, hi…." Her words died in her throat when she saw the girl's dazed appearance and my flushed face.

I knew what was going through her head, even though she guarded her expression well.

"I didn't expect to see you here," she said, "but I am glad because there was something I wanted to talk to you about. Are you free tonight?"

"Yes, I'm free." I tried to dislodge the girl's hand from my arm, but she was still half-conscious and stood stiffly, staring blankly ahead.

Brianna looked from the girl to me. A shadow crossed her features and the smile I had grown to expect was nowhere to be seen.

"Shall we do dinner, then? Say around six?" she said, her tone even and lacking warmth.

"Yes. Shall I call you when I am on my way?"

The girl was still holding onto my arm and it was becoming more awkward by the minute. Finally, I just turned to her and forcibly released her grip and moved away from her. She wandered off down towards the bookracks, leaving us alone.

"New friend?" Brianna asked.

I shook my head. "No, she was just having some dizziness and I helped her."

Brianna knew it was a lie. I could tell by the way her face fell, and I knew what she was assuming. I also understood it. In her position, I would assume the same thing. My thoughts sped as I tried to figure out how to make her understand the situation without also giving my secret away.

I took a step towards her. "We'll talk tonight. Shall we just get something to go and take it back to my house?"

Brianna just nodded silently, then turned on her heel and left without speaking another word. All I could do was watch her walk away. I could tell that she was very upset, but there was nothing I could do right then.

CHAPTER 12

Brianna said little on the way to get our food and was completely silent as we drove to my house. When we got inside, I busied myself setting the table and pouring wine. I hoped alcohol would ease the tension in the air.

We ate in silence. When she was finished, I poured more wine and we moved to the sitting room. She stared at the fire in the fireplace and did not look at me.

My heart felt like it would explode. "Brianna. It isn't what you think at all."

"Then what is it? Who is she? And is she the reason why you smell of someone else's perfume sometimes?"

"No."

Tears filled her eyes and two drops traveled slowly down her face. She brushed them away, trying hard to compose herself.

"Brianna, please." I touched her arm. "Please, just let me explain."

She looked at me, her features hard.

I searched desperately for the right words. "This is going to sound crazy and this is very difficult for me because I really love you and do not want to lose you. But I see no other thing to do and I know I should have told you before," I began, and then I told her what really happened to me that night in the village.

I told her about my immortality, and about what I must do to keep pain from crippling me. She sat quietly through my explanation and stared into the fire again towards the end. When I was done, I waited for her to look at me, but she did not move.

"I know you may not believe me, but I can prove it to you. I can show you." I got up to get a knife from the kitchen. When I returned she looked over at me.

"Koren, what are you doing?"

"I will prove it to you," I pulled up my shirtsleeve.

Brianna stood up. "No! You don't have to do that." She looked on in horror as I sliced a gash in my arm with the sharp blade.

"Oh god," she said.

"It's okay, my love, just watch."

The wound bled for just a moment and then a muted glow formed around my entire arm. When the glow disappeared, there was no sign of injury. Brianna looked up from my arm to meet my gaze, and then sat down.

"I'm sorry." It was all I could think of to say.

She began to cry, hard. Her whole body shook with the sobs. I sat down, feeling helpless and unsure what to do. Any other time I would have taken her into my arms but at that moment, I did not think she would want me close.

Then she looked over at me through tear-filled eyes. "Please," she said and reached out for my hand, and grasped it tightly. "Don't leave me now."

She came to me, into my arms and cried for a very long time as I held her. When she was too exhausted to shed any more tears, I picked her up, carried her to the bedroom, and put her to bed.

∞

In the morning when we had breakfast, Brianna seemed pensive and curious, but she did not seem so sad.

"Koren may I ask a question?"

"Of course."

"How exactly did the old woman make you what you are?"

"I was barely conscious, so I don't remember -- and it was so long ago I probably wouldn't remember the details even if I had been."

She looked down at the scrambled eggs on her plate and touched them with the tip of her fork. "Are you sure you don't remember? Or do you just not want to tell me?"

"Why wouldn't I want to tell you?"

"Because then maybe I'd try to become like you?"

"Why in the world would you want to be like me?"

"I am serious."

"I am, too. What she did to me… it is like some kind of disease, Brianna. I love you and yes, you are partly right. Even if I did know, I would not tell you. Any abilities I may have are not worth the curse of having to rely on others the way I do."

"We all rely on others for life, in one way or another."

"It isn't the same."

She stared down, stirring the eggs but not eating; finally, she placed the fork on the table and looked over at me, her expression soft. "I know you have held back in other ways from me sometimes, too, and I appreciate the reason, but you need to know that I would give you everything." She slid her hand atop mine. "You know that? I mean it. I would give you everything."

She stood and stepped around the table towards me to touch my face. Looking deeply into my eyes, she traced a finger down my jaw line and sat down on my lap, facing me.

"I would give you my life," she said quietly and planted soft kisses along the same path her finger had trailed moments before.

CHAPTER 13

I was surprised when I didn't hear from her that evening, but I tried not to worry and told myself that she was probably extra busy with grading. However, when I still had not received a phone call, email or text the next morning, I became concerned and decided to go by her office as I was already going to campus anyway.

The door was closed when I got there. I knocked softly and was relieved to hear her voice bid me to enter, but the relief vanished when I saw her. Something had changed. Her whole demeanor was stiff and her eyes lacked warmth.

"I hadn't heard from you, so I just thought I'd stop by to make sure you were okay." I tried to smile. "So, you are okay, right?"

She looked away and stood up, came around the desk to me. Her fingertips were cold on the back of my hand. "Not really." She looked into my eyes.

"Koren, please don't take this the wrong way."

My heart sank.

"It's been a strange week and I started thinking after our conversation." She looked away from me for a moment. I knew it was to gather courage. "I need some time, just a couple of days or so, to think. This has all gone so fast and my head is spinning."

I tried to keep my tone neutral when I said, "I understand," but it was not easy and I knew she could feel my sadness and disappointment.

"You... this has been so intense for me. But you have to know how I feel about you. Right? You know I love you...."

I could only nod. A part of me did understand. I felt horrible that we could not just have a normal relationship, and live like normal people. I did feel that she loved me, but I also knew how hard this probably was for her.

"I have just had a really normal life, I think, and this is so different now, and frankly scares me," she said. Her face flushed but it wasn't from embarrassment. I could tell she was trying not to cry. On one hand, I felt compassion. On the other hand, the hurt I felt brought feelings of anger and disgust. Disgust towards myself for being what I was. Disgust that she wasn't more trusting. Disgust that she would do this despite the sweet words she had said to me just the day before. I felt like a fool.

My throat was dry and I knew that if I did not leave her office soon, my real emotions would show. It was all I could do to keep my voice calm. I tried to remind myself that my anger wasn't with her, really. It was with the one who had interrupted our life hundreds of years ago.

"I do understand, Brianna. You know where to find me. Take the time you need."

Her expression darkened, turning sorrowful and she looked down at the floor. "I'm sorry… I just need to think and process this all," she said.

"Of course." I shrugged and headed towards the door.

"Koren…."

I turned to look back at her.

"I love you," she said.

∞

When I walked out of her office and out of the building, my mind scattered with emotions. The weight of the years was crushing down on me at last. After all this time, I had finally found her again only to have it destroyed.

People ambled past me. I wanted to push them. I wanted to grab them, shake them and scream at them to cherish their humanity, because everyone takes that for granted. Everyone wants to live forever but few understand that living right here, right now, embracing every moment of life, of love, is so much more valuable than living for years and years without the ability to really be with another human being. Everyone I ever loved died, or had to leave. Everyone.

I slowed my pace when it hit me that I could say the same thing to myself -- that I should embrace the moments. Closing my eyes, I clenched my teeth. I didn't have time nor desire for self-analysis at that moment.

Dark pain, suppressed for centuries, burned inside my chest. Steeling myself, I advanced through the corridor and out into glaring sunlight. The concrete walkways were filled with students. I pushed my way through them forcibly, without caring if I angered or offended. I had had enough.

At home, I fed Jasmine then sat down to decide what to do next. I would respect Brianna's wish and give her time, but I had little faith that she would choose to continue the relationship. And who in the world would blame her. I certainly did not.

CHAPTER 14

For the next two days, I kept myself busy to keep my mind off Brianna. I visited museums and shopping centers during the day and went to clubs at night. The hours after the clubs closed were the worst. Sleep was elusive and when I did sleep, I had nightmares about my loved ones Jona had burned alive.

On the third day, I was exhausted and my need for blood was unbearable, even though every day I had found someone to ease the ache. In addition to the hunger and exhaustion, I was depressed. I had decided that even if Brianna decided to stay with me, I could not allow it. I loved her. If I let her stay with me and finally lost control with her and hurt her, I would never forgive myself.

As the day turned into night, I turned to drinking. I hoped it would knock me out, but it only made me feel slightly tired.

Around eleven, I gave up and tried to sleep, but just as I closed my eyes, a breeze rushed through the room with such force that it toppled books from my bedside table. I sat up just as a foul odor filled the room and Jona's voice whispered through the darkness.

"You feel it, don't you Koren. It is almost over. Look at you now, so weak. The cravings, the pain, it will all get worse. Interesting, isn't it, how your cravings grew after you met Brianna. Perhaps it is because only her blood can sate you now. And each day that you refuse her gift, you will look worse, you will feel worse, until there is little left of you. What do you think she will think of you then? Do you think she will still want to be with you when you are so weak, so ravenous? Perhaps you will tear her throat open in a fit of hunger. You thought you cheated death, but really you have simply spent centuries waiting for the inevitable sorrow you knew had to come, isn't that right?"

His words got to me but I tried not to let it show. Rising from the bed, I stood in the middle of the room.

"Why don't you show yourself to me, Jona? Are you afraid? Perhaps you look so hideous it has made you shy. Or, maybe, maybe you cannot show yourself because you do not have enough strength. Yes, I think that is probably it, isn't it?"

"It will be soon, so soon. I look so forward to the look on your face when I kill her," Jona said, ignoring my questions.

Hearing those words, I froze.

Jona chuckled. "And then you will be next, of course. There won't be anyone around to save you this time."

"You can't kill me. You know that."

"Oh Koren. You are still so naïve. Of course I can kill you. There is a way. But, you will have to wait just a little while longer to find out how. It will be a surprise."

The room grew still and the odor vanished. Just as the times before, as quickly as he had arrived, he had gone.

I phoned Brianna, just to make sure she was okay and to warn her to be extra careful. This counted as an emergency and overrode our agreement to take a few days. She didn't answer and so I left a message on her voicemail, urging her to contact me, and decided that if she did not get back with me by the next day, I'd go check on her.

For the moment, I needed to go out and find someone before I felt weaker. If Jona were serious with the threats, I would need all the strength I could get. After slipping into a pair of jeans, boots, and a low cut blouse, I headed to the neighborhoods closer to the university.

∞

On most nights, one could find a party going on in the area and I was not disappointed. In an area full of student apartments and houses, dance music with a heavy, thumping rhythm split the peace of the evening.

I walked down the sidewalk, following the sound of the music to a fraternity house. One young man stood outside acting as a bouncer. I easily walked by him unnoticed.

Inside at least 30 college students stood around yelling over the music. Cigarette smoke mingled with the odor of beer. A few partiers were on the furniture, wrapped up in each other, making out. I was sure more had already found their way to the bedrooms upstairs and I knew it would not take me long to find several who would readily give me what I needed.

CHAPTER 15

The following morning, the sound of my doorbell startled me out of sleep. Pulling the blanket over my head, I tried to ignore it and willed the person to go away, but it continued. When I finally dragged myself out of bed and opened my door, Brianna stared back at me.

"I tried to call you back last night, and then again this morning, but you weren't answering the phone. I got worried," she said. "Are you okay? You don't look well."

By the time I had made it home the night before, most of the partiers had already passed out and birds had begun to chirp. Once home, I had fallen asleep in my clothes and I surely looked like hell and reeked of alcohol or worse.

"I'm fine, just a little tired."

Her expression let me know she didn't believe me but she didn't press it. She let me take her coat and then followed me into the sitting room. I asked her if she wanted anything to eat or drink.

She shook her head. "No, thank you… Hey, is this okay? Did I come at a bad time?"

"No, yes, of course it is okay."
We had barely sat down when she turned to me.

"I'm sorry for what I said; I just needed some time to process all that has happened."

Shrugging, I told her of course I understood, but I know she could tell that something was bothering me and that I was shutting off, a lot.

She touched my arm. "I really missed you."

When I said nothing, she continued. "I don't know how you feel now... maybe you changed your mind, for all I know, and I wouldn't blame you. But I really care about you and love you and although I must admit this all still really freaks me out and I don't understand what is really happening, I can't just let it go. I don't want to let it go. I want to be with you." She looked down at her hands. "No matter what."

I exhaled. At the sound, she looked over at me again, chewed her bottom lip, fear and hope battling each other across her features.

My concern for her safety was more important to me than the hurt I had felt and I did not waste time. "Brianna, I need to tell you some things that happened during the past three days."

I told her about the nightmares, and the most recent visit from Jona, because she needed to know, even though I was sure it would scare her. The color left her face as I described it all.

"I had something happen last night, too," she said. "I thought I was losing my mind. It was very quick, as if he just came and went almost as quickly, but I remember the odor and the breeze. I was up almost all night after that."

A twinge of guilt clutched my gut when I thought about where I had been all night.

After a pause she asked, "What do you think we should do?"

"I think this may only get worse, and I need to deal with him before it does. I am not sure what that entails, but I believe I need to go back to the place where this all began. My dreams have been very vivid and I think I need to listen to them. I leave it up to you whether or not you want to go with me. It needs to be your decision."

She looked down at her hands, nervously picked at her fingernails. "Well classes end in only two weeks. If we could wait until then, it would be easiest for me, but I understand if it needs to be sooner." Looking up at me, she continued. "I don't want you to go alone. I want to come with you. This involves us both."

∞

We spent most of the weekend together, needing the closeness, but unfortunately, just as Jona said would happen, my fatigue and craving worsened.

By Sunday night, Brianna couldn't keep her concern quiet anymore and asked me what was going on. I didn't know what to tell her, only that I thought it had something to do with Jona, which only made her more worried.

She became extra solicitous and loving towards me. Normally I would have delighted in this, but this time her behavior just underscored the fact that I was unwell. Sunday night she stayed, rather than going home as she usually would, unaware that her nearness was becoming torture when I hungered so. Nevertheless, after Jona's threats, I did not intend to let her spend nights alone.

CHAPTER 16

Monday morning she hadn't been gone more than an hour when she rang me from her office, crying so hard I could barely understand what she was saying. Finally, I deciphered that she was asking me to come quickly.

When I arrived and saw police cars and yellow crime scene tape around one of the buildings, my stomach churned. I hurried to her office and entered without knocking to find her crying quietly, her face buried in her hands.

"What happened?"

She stood and came to me, melting into my arms. "She was one of my students."

"Who? What happened?"

"Killed, murdered," she sobbed into my shoulder. I held her tightly, giving her time.

When she could speak again she told me that a girl had been found dead in a bathroom stall. I waited patiently as she choked on the next words. She looked at me. "The woman who found her was another student of mine. She said that her throat was ripped open."

A shudder ran through me when I realized what it could mean.

"Do you think Jona could have done that?" she asked.

I told her I did not know what he was capable of, but I had a feeling he had not been making empty threats.

"Could you take me home, love? I don't think I can drive right now."

I took her to my house and poured us glasses of wine while she washed her face in the bathroom. When she came out, she sat with me and leaned her head against my shoulder. Jasmine joined us, curling up next to Brianna as if she knew the woman needed extra comforting.

In the afternoon, while Brianna slept in my bed, I heard sounds outside my front door, sounds I assumed were the mail carrier. When I opened the door, there was no one there, and the mail hadn't come yet, but a piece of paper had been taped to my door. It was a note: *The girl at the university was just a delicious warm-up. See you soon.*

I glanced around, surveying the area. I knew the note's deliverer could not have made it far, but there was not a soul in sight. Stuffing the note in my pocket, I closed the door and locked it securely before checking all the other doors and windows in the home. I knew that a locked door could not keep Jona out, considering the powers he seemed to possess, but I wasn't going to give him an open invitation either.

Brianna slept until early evening. I waited for her to have a cup of tea and fully awaken before I told her about the note. She wondered aloud if we should still go to Scotland, considering what was going on. I told her that now, more than ever, we should, if only to lure him away from the campus. He would surely already know I was about to leave, and would follow.

CHAPTER 17

A cold breeze met us as we stepped outside Edinburgh airport. Brianna shivered next to me, but I knew it was not only from the cold. I put my arm around her as we waited for the car that would take us to Stonehaven.

During the drive, we were both tired and said little as we watched the landscape go by. That afternoon and evening, we would try to relax at a Bed and Breakfast and prepare for whatever was to come.

∞

Late in the morning the next day, I hired a driver to take us to the outskirts of town, to bring us closer to where I knew we needed to go. The scenery as we drove out of town was familiar, by both sight and sense. It was eerie for me to note how little some things had changed in all the years.

After a while, I saw familiar cliffs in the distance, and my heart thudded against my ribs.

Soon after that, we came to a fork in the road and I decided it was time to journey by foot.

"Here, please" I said to the driver.

He pulled over to the side and stopped the car. Looking back at us, he pointed to the right. "That road leads to forest and some ruins and not much else," he told us. "Are you sure you want off here? There are sure to be storms later, by the look of those clouds, and it is a long walk to any kind of shelter."

I pulled my cloak tightly around me and nodded as I opened the door. "Yes, I think we should be okay, but thank you."

Brianna got out of the car and looked at me, a trace of fear shadowing her eyes. I understood. I felt it too. As we watched the car drive away, I took her hand. "Are you ready?" She nodded silently and gripped my hand tightly.

∞

The dirt road we followed was well worn and I imagined all the many people who must have used it through the ages since I had been gone. It felt so strange to be back that I retreated into my own mind and had little to say. Brianna was also quiet. I was sure she could sense how life changing all of this could be for us.

We met no one along the way, until we came upon a small cluster of cottages. From a distance, we saw a human form standing outside of one of them. As we drew closer, we could see it was an old woman.

She stood in the front garden, with her back to us, and was so still, she could have been a statue. When we were nearly upon her, she turned and I froze.

Brianna looked at me but I was unable to look away from the steel grey eyes of the old woman, for they were familiar eyes.

"Hello, Koren. I knew you would come. I've been waiting for this day."

An icy breeze stirred and I shivered hard.

The woman turned her attention to Brianna and smiled. "And hello, dear Rowan. You look different now but I recognize you all the same."

Brianna dug her fingernails into my palm, bringing me out of my shock.

"Glenna?" I asked the woman.

She gave a simple nod. "It is too chilly to be standing out here when we could be inside having a hot cup of tea. Won't you two join me?"

We followed Glenna inside the modest cottage and sat at a small table as she began the preparations for tea. When she noted aloud that the fire in the hearth was dying down, I offered to bring in some kindling from outdoors.

I was gone only a few minutes, but when I returned, Brianna and the old woman were sitting closer together. They looked up at me in a way that made me believe I had interrupted a conversation. I wanted to ask about it but Glenna got up from the table without tarrying and began serving the tea.

We sat in silence for only a short while, but I soon grew anxious and impatient and it seemed as if hours were passing.

Finally, Glenna broke the silence. "I was very good friends with your mother and I still miss her terribly, Koren."

I pushed my cup and plate away and looked at her from across the table. "What did you do to me to make me as I am now and why?"

Brianna placed her hand on my leg under the table; she could hear the edge in my tone and it was a gesture meant to comfort me.

Glenna sat her cup of tea down. "I promised your mother I would keep you safe. Before Jona took her to the stake, she begged me to get you safely away from the village. I tried, but I failed, so I did what I could to keep you alive that night, so that someday you and Rowan would find each other again."

"I am not really alive. This is not natural. Neither are you. It has been over 600 years. I've not aged a minute since that night."

"But it was meant to be, Koren. You and Rowan were meant to be. Only Jona's evil interfered with that, with what was meant to be. I tried to correct what--."

"*Correct*?" I stood now, suddenly furious and unable to calm myself. Brianna looked up at me with troubled eyes, but remained seated, unsure what she could do for me as I continued. "I'm some kind of fucking freak!"

The room grew still. Glenna folded her hands in front of her and looked at them pensively before lifting her gaze to me again. "You are alive, Koren."

My anger was not satisfied. "But at what price to others! What kind of life, to have to pull life energy from others this way. What kind of life, to watch everyone I care about grow old and die while I live on, and on."

"Look at her, Koren," she nodded towards Brianna, "Is finding her not reward enough?"

I slammed my fist onto the table in front of the old woman. "You know that is *not* what I mean!"

She simply looked into my eyes. "What would you have me do, Koren?"

Overwhelmed with emotion, I looked away and slumped back down into the chair. I needed to think, to gather myself together somehow. Brianna sat very quietly, but I sensed her deep sorrow and compassion, reaching out to me.

Finally, I looked up again. "I would have you help me destroy Jona, forever. So that we may at last, live in peace." I said.

Glenna moved her cup aside and pushed herself slowly up from the table. Without a word, she walked to the other side of the room and stopped before a black trunk. From it, she withdrew something wrapped in a black cloth. She returned, cradling the object and placed it in the middle of the table. Casting me the briefest of glances, she removed the cloth covering.

It was a sword, Jona's sword. The one he had plunged into me. The old woman wordlessly unsheathed it and placed it in front of me. The blade shined. It had been cared for well.

"This is the only thing that can end his life, and only if you are the one wielding it. The night he tried to take your life, the sword was just a simple sword. But with Rowan's vow to you, your innocent blood on the blade, and my oath to your mother... it became infused with new power. It is a gateway of sorts."

New understanding hit me at that moment. "You made Jona what he is now. He was mortal in the past. He reincarnated before, but never did he have the powers he has now," I said.

"Yes. It was the only way I could make sure you would come back to this place. Because of what I did for you that night, my fate has been tied to yours thereafter, Koren. The very moment that you and Rowan reconnected, I knew about it. Now it is time for me to go. I can be released now." Her voice faltered. "I am very tired. You, you were still young but I was already old and have been trapped in this old body all of these years. Only you can release me. Only you can kill me, and only on this land and only with this sword."

I arose from the table again, my anger exploding. "You put us through all of this just so I would come here and *kill* you?"

"I did not realize just how strong he would become, Koren. It was a terrible mistake but I have lived only to see this day, to see you and Rowan together again." Tears shone in the old woman's eyes. "Please forgive me."

Brianna touched my arm, tearing my attention away. Her blue eyes were full of pain. I could tell she wanted so much to speak, to calm me, but she could not find the words. Much of my anger melted away under her touch and gaze alone.

Exhaling slowly, I touched her hair. "Brianna, maybe it would be better if you wait outside for a little while."

CHAPTER 18

Outside the cottage, Brianna sat against a stone wall. Her eyes met mine and held as I walked out. We didn't need to say anything. She knew by the look in my eyes that I had granted the old woman her final wish. She stood up as I neared, and then wrapped her arms around me tightly and held on to me for a long time.

When she did finally pull away, fresh tears shimmered in her eyes. As one traveled slowly down her cheek, I gently brushed it away with my thumb. "We could go back to the hotel, rest up and come back tomorrow," I told her softly.

She shook her head. "No. We are here, now. The sooner we do whatever we have to do, the sooner we can go back home and move on with life, right?"

My heart clenched so hard I had to glance away. How could I tell her now, after all we had been through, that I believed my poor condition would get worse, and not better, after destroying Jona. Battling him would take all the strength I had left. I was not sure I would be going home, or anywhere, afterwards.

She pressed her palm to my face, guiding me to look at her. "I'm ready, Koren. To say I am not frightened would be a lie. But I know we must go through with this or we may never have peace."

Silently, I pulled away from her to enter the cottage and retrieve the sword.

∞

Several miles down, the road veered to the left. There, an overgrown trail led from the road into the trees. I sensed that following that trail would bring us to the ruins of the village we once called home. After making sure the sword and sheath were still tied securely to my belt, I grasped Brianna's hand and led us through the forest.

Brambles and tall weeds slowed our progress, but before long, we could see a clearing through an opening in the trees. Brianna stopped abruptly as we grew nearer and caught the first sight of the village. She squeezed my hand tightly. I could feel her trembling and knew memories were coming back to her, more strongly than ever. A cold breeze blew through the forest, making her tremble harder.

"A lot more is left than I expected," I said.

Nature had destroyed the old thatch roofs, but the stone walls of the buildings remained, including the walls of Jona's cottage. My stomach tightened, noting this.

In addition, although weeds had grown up to cover most passageways, the ground in the center of the village was barren, as if in memory of the burning pyres that once covered it.

Brianna shivered again and I looked at her. "Are you okay?"

"I just didn't expect it to feel so familiar," she said.

I nodded, understanding.

The breeze died as we stepped into the village, the stillness a sharp contrast to the sound of our breathing. Brianna kept hold of my hand and slowly we made our way to what remained of Jona's cottage.

We paused at the entrance. I thought of that night, so long ago, and how Rowan had sacrificed herself, hoping to give me a chance to survive. I tightened my grip on Brianna's hand to keep her close.

"This was where he tried to kill me," I said, although I knew she already sensed it.

I stepped over the threshold, taking her with me. The stone walls felt like a tomb surrounding us. It looked so different, so exposed, without the thatched roof covering it, but so many things had somehow survived the centuries. The hearth in the middle of the room sagged; the stones lay scattered around as if crushed by the heaviness of the sky itself. An iron cauldron lay where it fell, unmoved for centuries. A wood table had oddly resisted rotting away, as well as a chair nearby. I paused, feeling cold fear settle in my belly. It was the chair he had sat me on that night. I looked to the spot I had lain, bleeding. The floor there was bare.

At last I spoke, only because the silence was too much. "I thought more would have changed in all these years."

Brianna shuddered next to me. "Koren...."

An icy breeze blew over us followed by the shuffling sound of footsteps over the hard-packed dirt floor. We could not see him, but we both felt him. Quickly, I grabbed Brianna and pulled her towards the doorway.

"Brianna, run! Get out!"

Her eyes widened but she simply clung to me more tightly and didn't move.

"Please, trust me and get out now!"

She hesitated for only a breath more before running from the cottage.

CHAPTER 19

When I moved back away from the doorway, Jona appeared before me as if he had been there all along. He reeked of decay and the odor wrapped around me like a noose, making me gag. He looked past me to watch Brianna running in the distance, and chuckled low in his throat before turning his attention to me. He stared at me for a long moment. It was enough time for me to see that whatever powers he possessed, they weren't enough to make him appear fully human or alive. His skin was the mottled grey of a long-dead corpse. His eyes were sunken, dark and opaque.

My heart pounded against my ribs as he continued to stare, but I did not move.

"You want to kill me, Koren. Yes." He took a step closer. "But, of course, you know I will not let you."

I held my ground and did not flinch from his dark gaze.

He grinned, displaying a mouth full of rotting teeth. "The old woman thought she was saving you by making you an immortal that night, so long ago. But dying then would have been far more pleasant than what I have planned for you now."

He took another step towards me. With each movement of his cloak, the stench of death grew stronger; my stomach churned and I gagged again. Impatient with my silence, Jona continued to walk towards me. Discretely, I moved my hand beneath my cloak, closer to the hilt of the sword.

Another cold breeze swept through the cottage. Jona's hood fell back, exposing greasy black hair that hung around his face, dangling like thin wet worms.

I wanted to flee, but steeled myself to buy Brianna extra time to get far away, in case Jona decided to go after her. "You said you loved me then, Jona. But what kind of love wants to torture and kill their beloved?"

A laugh tore from his throat. "Love? Oh I once loved you .Yes, yes, once upon a time. And what a fool I was for that. But I am no fool now."

He lunged towards me, faster than I could react, grabbed me by the throat with a cold hand, and squeezed. The moment his fingers touched me, I felt energy drain from me. As he tightened his grip, I had to fight to retain consciousness.

Black eyes bore into mine, his rancid breath assaulting me as he spat each word. "I will kill that girl you think you love. I will make you watch as I drain the life slowly from her pathetic little mortal body. You will watch it all, knowing you brought her here to me, to suffer the fate due to her centuries ago. A fate she escaped only by killing herself."

"And then, Koren, then, I will make you beg for mercy that will never come."

With one shove, he sent me sprawling over the hard floor, and then he turned briskly towards the doorway, his form fading in and out of view.

Enraged, I screamed and lunged at him. He shook me off effortlessly, then grabbed me by the shoulders and flung me against the stone hearth. My head cracked against the iron cauldron. Blood soaked my hair immediately and I blacked out for a moment.

Jona could have left then to seek Brianna, but his hatred towards me needed to be sated first. I regained consciousness as his booted foot met my jaw, then my chest. The wound to my head was already healing, but his presence was draining so much power from me that I felt the pain of each new blow fully. He kicked me in the stomach, repeatedly, until I vomited blood. When my pain was finally severe enough to appease his rage, he ran out the doorway without looking back.

I stumbled out of the cottage only a few moments later, but Jona had already reached the forest at the edge of the village. Gritting my teeth against the jolts of pain ripping through my belly, I forced my limbs to move in pursuit. I could only pray that the time I spent fighting him had given Brianna enough of a chance to find a hiding place.

Leaves and twigs cracked like bones beneath my feet as I scrambled through the forest. Jona looked back at me and growled. He paused, and seemed to consider going back to fight me again, but then turned to continue running.

To my dismay, he then began to fade from my sight – not by gaining ground, but by using whatever power he possessed to make himself invisible. Soon I could hear him but not see him, except for brief glimpses when his power faltered. I had to rely on the sound of his footsteps and my intuition.

The sword at my side beat against my leg with each stride. My love for Brianna urged me on, over-riding my pain and exhaustion and lending strength to muscle, sinew and bone. Up ahead, Jona moved erratically, attempting to throw me off his trail. I followed his sounds through a narrow passage and stumbled over stones and vines. Branches clawed at my cloak and pulled the cord taut around my neck. Furiously, I grasped at the material until I tugged myself free.

Meanwhile, Jona had gained more distance; however his power to remain unseen faded as he neared a clearing ahead, where the forest gave way to the grassy cliffs. It was then that I also spotted Brianna. She was crouched behind a boulder, hidden from Jona's view.

My breath caught as I watched him stop just a few feet away from her, as if he knew. Frantic to draw his attention away from the boulder, I emerged from the trees and shouted out to him. "It's too late for you, Jona!"

I hoped he would turn to me; instead, he laughed and took a slow step towards Brianna's hiding place. He knew she was there.

"Brianna, run!" I screamed as I ran towards him. She darted out and sprinted away but in a direction that took her closer to the cliff edge. Ignoring me, Jona ran after her and quickly closed in.

Brianna looked to me, her eyes wide with terror. My heart froze.

"Get away from the edge!" I screamed at her.

Jona slowed his pace but continued to advance towards her. "Oh no, Rowan. You won't be escaping me this time."

I finally reached him and threw myself upon him to pull him back only one terrifying moment before he grabbed her.

We fell to the ground together and rolled, each struggling for control of the other. I clawed his face and shoved my knee into his groin, but nothing seemed to affect him. He only grunted before punching me in the face and pushing off me to chase Brianna, who had darted away.

The moment he turned his back, I was on my feet after him, drawing the sword as I ran. The metallic sound of the blade against the sheath's metal band drew his attention.

He twisted around just in time for me to shove the sword into his torso.

His mouth gaped open in a scream that never sounded. Bewilderment spread over his features. He shook his head, looked to the sky and crumpled to the earth. I held tightly to the sword's hilt even as he fell and pulled it out only to thrust it deep into his heart as he stared up at me.

Dark, rancid blood spilled from his body and seeped into the grass as his body jerked one final time.

CHAPTER 20

Brianna had witnessed everything from several yards away. She moved a little closer to me now, but the way she stared at Jona's body, I could tell she was in a state of shock.

"It's okay. He's dead," I said. She looked up from the body to me and then down to the bloody sword in my hand. I wiped it clean on the grass and went to her, to wrap her in a tight embrace. After a few moments I pulled back to look into her eyes and make sure she was okay. Her expression was still distant.

I brushed loose strands of hair back from her face with my fingertips and spoke to her quietly. "I want to take the body back to the village and burn it. I want to be sure there is no way he can come back in this form."

She nodded and followed me back to Jona's body.

As I stood looking down at him again, my knees weakened. The power that had helped me fight him was fading and the exhaustion and pain that had become so common to me was returning. I wasn't sure how I would manage to drag him back in my current state; nevertheless, I didn't want Brianna to have to touch him. When she asked how she could help me, I told her I would handle him myself.

It took me over half an hour, but we finally made it back to the ruins and, once there, I deposited Jona's corpse in the village center. Brianna then quietly helped me gather wood and form a pyre next to him.

After I had lifted the body and set it on top, I told Brianna she should walk a ways into the forest so she did not have to watch the burning.

She shook her head. "No, I want to stay with you."

I understood why she did not want to go. I knew she was still shaken, but I preferred she not have to witness the flames, and I told her so.

She shook her head again and drew closer to me. "I understand, love, but I don't want to be alone right now." Her eyes searched mine until I nodded to her, to let her know I understood.

I opened the small satchel that held our emergency supplies and lit several of the matches to place in the dry tinder. The fire roared quickly to life; the flames licked hungrily at the wood and then the body. We walked at least one hundred yards upwind to avoid the smoke and odor, but it followed us nevertheless.

As I stood watching to make sure the fire did not get out of control, Brianna pressed her face to my shoulder and began to cry.

∞

My exhaustion worsened as the fire blazed. By the time the flames had died down, I felt so dizzy and weak I could barely remain standing. I stepped away from Brianna when my legs started to buckle. Although I struggled to right myself, I fell hard. The sword broke away from my belt on impact and clattered loudly across the ground to rest several feet away.

Brianna knelt quickly by my side. "What happened? What's wrong?"

"I should have told you," I said.

"What do you mean? Should have told me what?" Her hand fluttered to my forehead, then my cheek. Worry creased her forehead.

I tried to breathe evenly, but something was happening to me. Something very bad. "I'm very unwell."

"What? Koren, I don't understand."

"And I fear I could hurt you." I swallowed and tried to take a deep breath. "This is just going to get worse." I paused again. My lungs felt like they were about to explode. "Please forgive me and try to understand. I cannot bear the thought that one day I might get carried away with you. There is only one thing I can think of to do now to prevent that."

Brianna shook her head, not understanding.

"I cannot go on like this, and you deserve so much more," I said, before a sharp pain forced a cry from my throat. It felt like someone was plunging hot daggers into my bones.

Brianna looked into my eyes. "What? To do what?" You are saying you want to die?" Tears sprang to her eyes. "Koren, please tell me why? Why do you want to die now, Jona is dead. We can live out our lives in peace."

"Brianna, the girl, your student…."

She shook her head slowly, saying "No, you won't tell me you killed her, because I won't believe you."

"Jona killed her. But it could have just as well have been me if this continues. It is what I fear could happen." Saying the words, admitting the fear, made me feel I would vomit.

I took a moment to compose myself then looked up into her eyes. "Please help me. I don't know if I have the strength left to do it myself."

Her face bore the horror of what I was saying. "What? Koren, what are you asking?"

I looked at the sword where it lay. "Brianna…."

"Oh god." She shook her head. "How can you even ask this? I love you! I can't kill you!"

Lucidity returned to me briefly and I realized how cruel a request it was. "I'm so sorry, my love. I thought killing Jona might ease the weakness and the craving that has overtaken me the past few months. But look at me. Can you not see what is happening to me?"

Brianna shook her head. Her hot tears fell on my cheeks. "I can help you. We can... there must be something we can do, some way to make you well again."

I shook my head. "Brianna, I know there is nothing --." I paused because her expression had suddenly changed. She looked away from me and stared into the distance.

"I know what to do. The old woman told me," she said.

"What?"

"When you went outside to get the firewood she told me things."

Understanding hit me. "Brianna, no! You don't know what a price that is to pay and you know I won't let you do it!"

She ignored me, stood up and began to pace, wringing her hands, her whole body shaking. Tears slid in a continuous stream down her cheeks. "I can't lose you now. I don't want to lose you again. No." She shook her head.

"Brianna, Look at me! Look at what I have become!"

She looked at me. "I love you. How can you ask this? And how can you not understand why I cannot let you kill yourself?" She looked over at the sword, "and certainly not when I know how to help you."

In that moment, I realized what she was planning. With a cry, I struggled to reach the sword before she did, but she was faster. Holding the sword with both hands, she stepped back from me, her gaze fixed on me. Her hands trembled.

"I love you," she said before plunging the tip of the blade into her neck, as I watched, helpless and horrified. Blood gushed from the wound when she withdrew the sword and then she collapsed upon me. The hot crimson fountain poured from her, over my face and into my mouth. I tried to scream but her blood filled my throat.

Darkness pulled me down as I lost consciousness. Dreams and visions followed, full of lost days of beauty and innocence, of walking through the forests and near the cliffs together, long before we ever knew tragedy. And then the beautiful images vanished and I felt like I was falling. Panic clawed me, urging me to fight my way back to consciousness, to try to save Brianna.

It was not to be. Instead, we succumbed to our new fate, with her humanity, her life force, filling me.

∞

Storm clouds had darkened the sky when I finally awoke. Brianna was draped over me, her breath coming in weak, uneven gasps. My shirt was soaked with her blood. As gently as I could, I turned her over, on to her back and quietly spoke her name. She moaned.

"Brianna, open your eyes. Can you do that for me?" Thunder rumbled overhead, competing with my words, but she heard me and blinked up at me.

She blinked again, trying to focus. I knew her vision was blurred, for she had lost so much blood. I also knew that she would recover and she would not die, for she now shared my curse.

"I'm sorry, Koren."

"It will be okay," I said.

Sadness darkened her eyes. "I couldn't just let you die."

Drawing her tightly to me, I sat up to rock her slowly in my arms. "Don't try to talk right now. Save your strength, my love."

As she relaxed against me, I pressed my own wrist to my mouth and bit through the thin skin. I held it to her lips and watched as she tentatively tasted the blood and then began to suck hungrily.

Grief exploded inside me watching this simple act. A sob clenched my throat and tears rolled down my face as the weight of Brianna's sacrifice crashed over me in waves. I closed my eyes to the sight and held her more tightly to me, praying for help from whichever gods might hear me.

We were both changed forever. Nothing would ever be the same. Her action had healed me and united us fully as one, but at such a terrible price for her. Fresh tears wrenched from me and I wanted to scream.

Brianna pulled away from my wrist and reached one hand up to brush the tears from my cheeks. "Please don't cry, my love, "she said, "We will be together forever now."

Thunder rolled across the sky again and soon the rain began to fall. The drops dripped from my hair, down my face, mixing with my tears until I had no more tears left. I held Brianna throughout the storm and we let the rain pour over us, let it cleanse us.

∞ ∞

ABOUT THE AUTHOR

Chris M. Carmichael believes in love. She also believes in shiny swords and people who can kick butt. She loves going back to her fiction roots to explore new worlds and characters, and uncover hidden treasures within the human mind.

In addition to writing, Chris enjoys long walks in dark forests with things that go bump in the night.